THE COMMON COLD

ELAINE LANDAU

Marshall Cavendish
Benchmark
New York

Marshall Cavendish Benchmark
99 White Plains Road
Tarrytown, New York 10591
www.marshallcavendish.us

Expert Reader: Leslie L. Barton, M.D., professor of pediatrics, University of Arizona College of Medicine,
Tucson, Arizona

Library of Congress Cataloging-in-Publication Data
Landau, Elaine.
The common cold / by Elaine Landau.
  p. cm. — (Head-to-toe health)
Summary: "Provides basic information about the common cold and its prevention"—Provided by publisher.
Includes bibliographical references and index.
ISBN 978-0-7614-2844-2
1. Cold (Disease)—Juvenile literature. I. Title.
RF361.L36 2009
616.2'05—dc22
                              2007035005

Editor: Christine Florie
Publisher: Michelle Bisson
Art Director: Anahid Hamparian
Series Designer: Alex Ferrari

Photo research by Connie Gardner

Cover photo by Creatas/Jupiter Images

The photographs in this book are used by permission and through the courtesy of:
PhotoEdit: Michael Newman, 4; *Corbis:* Richard Hutchings, 6; Ariel Skelley, 15, 26; Chris Collins, 19; *Photo Researchers Inc.:* James Cavallini, 7; A. Barry Dowsett, 9; Eye of Science, 12; *Getty Images:* Science Faction, 10; Peter Cade, 16; *Phototake:* George Kelvin, 11; *The Image Works:* John Birdsall, 21; *Digital Railroad:* John Greim/Mira, 23; *Alamy:* Norbert Schaefer, 25.

Printed in China
1 3 5 6 4 2

CONTENTS

AH . . . CHOO!

You know the signs. It's winter, and it's really cold. Lots of people around you are getting sick. The girl sitting next to you at school has a bad cough. Your little brother has a runny nose. The kid behind you on the bus keeps sneezing. Last week your teacher was out sick, too.

All these people have something in common. They have a common illness known as the common cold.

The common cold is not a serious illness. But it can make you feel rotten. You've probably

BRRRRRR . . . WINTER WEATHER

Winter is known as the common cold season. There is a reason for this. In cold weather people tend to stay indoors. Often they are around other people, so cold germs have more of a chance to spread.

◄ **A sneeze is one of the first signs that a cold is coming on.**

A cold can make you feel run down and tired.

had colds in the past. Most school-age children get six to ten colds a year.

Remember what having a cold is like? You cough and sneeze. Sometimes you have a runny nose and watery eyes. Other times you just feel stuffed up. You may have a sore throat as well. Many people with colds feel tired and achy. Their voices are hoarse. They may have headaches and fever, too.

Luckily you do not stay sick for very long when you have a cold. Cold **symptoms** usually only last for about one to two weeks. It's great to feel better again.

THE INVADERS ARRIVE

Oh, no . . . you've got a cold. You feel like aliens have invaded your body. In a way they have. These aliens aren't from outer space, though. They are extremely tiny germs known as **viruses**.

THE VIRUS INVADERS

There are many different kinds of viruses. All are too tiny to be seen with the naked eye. Viruses are among the smallest germs on Earth. About 300 billion viruses could fit on the head of a pin.

More than two hundred viruses cause colds. Our bodies cannot build up a defense against

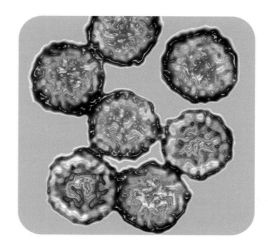

These are common cold viruses as seen through an electron microscope.

or resistance to that many viruses. That's why we keep getting colds caused by different viruses.

COLD QUIZ

How much do you know about the common cold? Can you complete this sentence? A rhinovirus is:

(a) an 8,000-pound animal with one or two large horns on its nose.
(No, that's a rhinoceros.)
(b) a very shiny piece of glass or paste made to look like a gemstone.
(No, that's a rhinestone.)
(c) a type of cold virus that grows best at 91 degrees Fahrenheit.
(That's the temperature inside the human nose.)
C is the right answer. Rhinoviruses make up about 35 percent, or one-third, of the viruses that cause colds. Some scienists say they are the leading cause of the common cold.

THE INVADERS AT WORK

Even though viruses are very small, they can still make you feel very sick. Cold viruses thrive in the tissues that line your nose and throat. There a virus attaches itself to a cell. Then it works its way into the cell. Once inside, the virus multiplies. It makes more and more copies of itself.

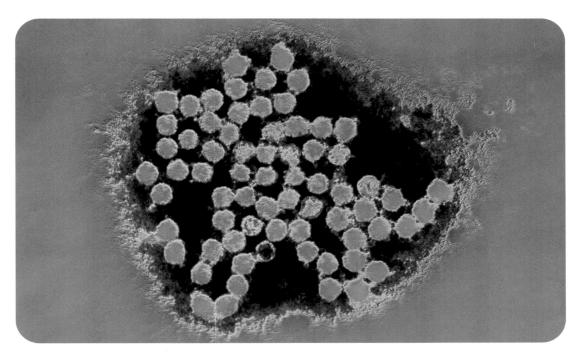

Cold viruses invade a cell, which will burst when full.

Before long the cell is filled with viruses. Think about what happens when you blow up a balloon. It fills with air. If you keep blowing, the balloon will burst. Something like that happens as a cell fills with viruses. It bursts open, and the viruses inside spill out.

These viruses invade other cells. Cold viruses are fast workers. In a single day as many as ninety million viruses can be made in your nose and throat. When you sneeze or cough, you release some of these germs. Small droplets containing the virus are sprayed into the air.

About 20,000 of these droplets are released in a single sneeze! Some scientists think that these germs may stay in the air for as long as half an hour. You can't see them—they are like an invisible haze.

These germs travel on air currents as well. When someone with a cold coughs or sneezes, germs can travel up to 12 feet. That's clear across a small room!

Thousands of germs, as well as mucus and saliva, are released into the air in a single sneeze.

HELP IS ON THE WAY

You may feel like resting when you have a cold. However, your body isn't really resting. It is working hard to fight off the virus. One way it does this is by producing special proteins called **antibodies**. These stop the virus from attaching itself to healthy cells.

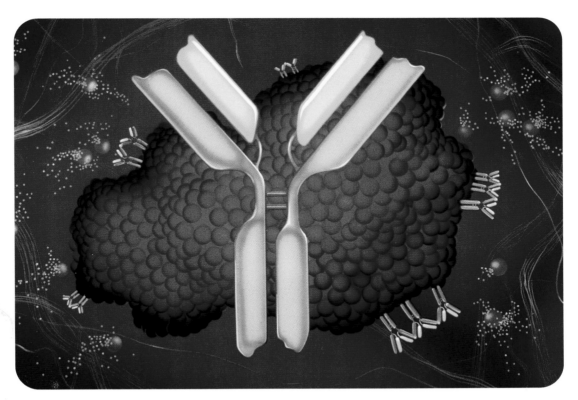

Antibodies, the Y-shaped objects, attach themselves to a virus and stop it from attaching to a healthy cell.

WARNING TO COLD GERMS— DON'T ENTER HERE

Did you know that your body has special barriers to protect you from cold germs? The lining of your nose is covered with tiny, hairlike structures called **cilia** (below). These help keep cold germs out. The skin inside your nose is covered with a sticky substance called **mucus**. It traps cold viruses, too.

Your throat has its own cilia and layer of mucus. These are great at trapping cold viruses. Sometimes germs that are caught in your throat are pushed out when you sneeze!

Your body produces other substances to fight the cold virus as well. Some of these germ fighters can give you a sore throat, achy muscles, and a runny nose. You probably thought it was the virus that was making you feel so sick. Actually, it was your body's defenses fighting those germs!

Your body's defenses serve as soldiers in the war against germs. When germs attack, they spring into action. It is their job to protect you and they do it well. In a way, they are your body's superheroes.

GERMS SPREAD TO YOUR HEAD

Cold symptoms don't show up right away. You can be around a bunch of people who have colds and still feel great the next day. Then, two or three days later, your nose may start to feel irritated. Sometimes a scratchy throat is the first symptom. Before long you start sneezing, and your head feels stuffy.

GERMS–HERE, THERE, AND EVERYWHERE

Colds are highly **contagious**. You can catch a cold in different ways. Sometimes the person standing next to you coughs or sneezes. When that happens, **airborne** germs are given off in tiny droplets. You can get sick by breathing in those germs. There are other ways to catch a cold as well.

One way to catch a cold is by touching something that already has cold germs on it.

You can also catch a cold by touching an object or surface that has germs on it. Let's say that a boy with a cold goes to the playground with his friends. He has a runny nose but forgets to bring along his tissues. A few times that afternoon he wipes his nose with his hand. During that time the boy remains

A COLD IS NOT THE FLU

Do you think that there's no difference
between the common cold and the flu? Think again.
Here are just a few of the differences.
With the flu you usually have a high fever and sometimes chills. When
you have a cold, you have either a low fever or no fever at all.
With a common cold you feel stuffy and sneeze a lot. If you have the flu,
your head feels clear, and there's little sneezing.
People with the flu often feel extremely achy and very tired.
Those with colds feel less achy and are not as exhausted.

with his friends at the playground. He pitches a ball and holds a bat. Both the ball and bat now have the boy's germs on them.

The boy also buys a hot dog at a food stand. He tears off half of the hot dog and gives it to his best friend. When he tears the hot dog in two, the boy still has not washed his hands.

What if you were with that boy at the playground? You threw the ball after he did, and you used the same bat. You were the person who shared his hot dog. When you touched these things, the germs could have gotten on your hands. Then you might have touched your nose or mouth before you washed your hands. In a few days you may be sneezing, too.

The same sort of thing happens when people with germs on their hands touch telephones, staircase railings, computer keyboards, light switches, toilet handles, bathroom faucets, or doorknobs. Cold viruses are passed on, and other people get sick.

How to Feel Better When You Have a Cold

Over the years medical science has come a long way. Today many illnesses can be cured. However, the common cold is not one of them.

This may be partly because so many different viruses cause the common cold. All of the viruses that cause colds may not even be known yet. In any case, it's doubtful that one **vaccine** could be developed to protect people against all of these viruses.

LONG, LONG AGO

Nevertheless, people have searched for a cure through the ages. The ancient Romans had some interesting ideas about how to cure colds. They believed that kissing the nose of a hairy mouse could help.

Today we know much more about the common cold. We know that there are things you can do to feel better. Some people find the cold medicines sold at drugstores helpful.

They may not be tasty, but certain cold medicines can make you feel better.

DID
YOU
KNOW?

A person with a cold is most contagious during the first two to three days. By the seventh to tenth day most people with colds are no longer contagious. Then it's safe for them to be out and about with friends.

These pills and syrups will not stop or shorten your cold. Yet sometimes, they can lessen your symptoms. That can make you feel a lot better.

However, you must be careful when taking these medicines. Never take anything for your cold that isn't given to you by the adult caring for you. Many of these over-the-counter drugs are not meant for children. For children under the age of six, over-the-counter medicines shouldn't be given at all. It is also important that the proper **dose** be taken.

There are other measures you can take to feel better, too. It's a good idea to get plenty of rest while you are sick. Your body needs to be in good shape to fight those cold germs.

Drink lots of fluids while you're sick. When you have a cold, your body loses fluid. You want to replace this. Try drinking a glass of juice or having a cup of broth or some Jell-O every two hours.

Some people say that a bowl of hot soup or tea with honey and lemon can do wonders to soothe a sore throat. If

A good way to take care of yourself when you have a cold is by drinking plenty of fluids.

your throat feels especially scratchy or sore, try gargling with warm saltwater. This often brings some relief.

Have you ever heard the saying "Time cures everything"? Although that's not true for all illnesses, it is true for the common cold. When you have a cold and feel really miserable, remember this: it won't be long before your cold is gone!

Staying Well

Nobody likes having a cold. But there's some good news. Armed with some helpful hints, you may be able to get fewer colds. When it comes to avoiding cold viruses, a little **prevention** can go a long way.

AVOIDING COLD GERMS

How do you keep cold germs from spreading? One way is easier than you think. It's something you've been doing since you were young—washing your hands.

Washing your hands is extremely important. Today, many scientists think that most colds are spread through touch. Remember to wash your hands whenever you use the bathroom as well as when you come home from school. Be sure to wash your hands before you eat.

DO YOU KNOW HOW TO WASH YOUR HANDS?

Everyone answers yes to this question.
However, many people do not wash their hands
properly. Here's what to do:
first wet your hands with warm water and apply soap. Work up a lather
by rubbing your hands together. Scrub your palms as well as the outer sides
of your hands. Clean beneath your fingernails, too. The soap,
along with the scrubbing, helps get rid of the germs.
Try not to rush. Most people don't spend enough time at the sink. You should
be able to sing the "Happy Birthday" song twice before you are finished.

Also avoid touching your eyes, nose, or mouth before washing your hands. You may have germs on your hands and not know it. Try not to bite your finger nails for the same reason.

Bring a gel hand cleanser or wipes with you on outings. These are ideal if you're not going to be near a sink for a while. They contain alcohol, which kills germs instantly. You don't even need water or a towel to use these gels.

MORE TIPS FOR STAYING HEALTHY

Eat right and get plenty of rest. Remember to have some foods that are high in vitamin C. These include oranges, grapefruits, and peaches, among others. You want to keep your **immune system** in tip-top shape. That helps your body fight off cold germs.

Do not share foods that you eat with your hands with anyone who has a cold. It doesn't matter if that person is your brother, sister, or best friend. It has nothing to do with liking the person. This is about staying healthy. Use a separate towel when drying your hands as well. Paper towels are a good choice, too.

Did a friend who has a cold come over to your house? What if someone in your family has a cold? It's a good idea to

Sharing food that you eat with your hands spreads germs.

use a **disinfectant** on the phone, computer keyboard, or other items that the sick person used. This can help you get rid of germs before those germs get to you!

No one wants you to become a **hermit** during the cold season. But it's wise to try to avoid large crowds during this time. Remember that the common cold is highly contagious. When you are around a lot of people, you are more likely to get sick.

Of course, these tips are not foolproof. You can follow them and still get a cold. Nevertheless, you will have increased your chances of staying well.

Avoiding colds can help make the winter months much more pleasant. Hopefully, next winter the word *cold* will have a completely different meaning for you. You'll only be using it to describe the weather!

Stay healthy and active during the winter by eating right, getting plenty of rest, and washing your hands frequently.

GLOSSARY

airborne — traveling through the air

antibodies — special proteins produced by the body to fight germs

cilia — tiny, hairlike structures that help keep cold germs out of the body

contagious — able to be spread by direct contact

disinfectant — a chemical used to kill germs

dose — a measured amount of medicine

hermit — someone who lives alone and avoids all contact with other people

immune system — the system that protects the body against disease

mucus — a sticky substance produced by the body to protect it

prevention — stopping something from happening

symptoms — the outward signs of an illness

vaccine — a substance injected into the body that protects against a disease

viruses — tiny germs that are too small to be seen without a special microscope

FIND OUT MORE

BOOKS

Glaser, Jason. *Colds*. Mankato, MN: Capstone Press, 2005.

Goldstein, Natalie. *Viruses*. New York: Rosen, 2004.

Mitchell, Melanie. *Killing Germs*. Minneapolis: Lerner, 2006.

Nye, Bill and Kathleen W. Zoehfeld. *Bill Nye the Science Guy's Great Big Book of Tiny Germs*. New York: Hyperion, 2005.

Sherman, Josepha. *The War Against Germs*. New York: Rosen, 2004.

Verdick, Elizabeth. *Germs Are Not for Sharing*. Minneapolis: Free Spirit Publishing, 2006.

DVDS

All About Health & Hygiene (The Human Body For Cildren). Schlessinger Media, 2006.

Body Mechanics: Superheroes of the Human Body. Library Video Company, 2006.

Nutrition (Health For Children). Schlessinger Media, 2005.

Personal Health & Hygiene (Health for Children). Schlessinger
    Media, 2005.

WEB SITES

What Are Germs?

www.kidshealth.org/kid/talk/qa/germs.html

Visit this Web site to learn how germs affect our health.

Be a Germ Stopper

www.cdc.gov/germstopper/

Check out this Web site to learn more about how you can keep
yourself healthy.

Meet the Scrub Club

www.scrubclub.org

Learn how to combat germ villians through the fun games on this
Web site.

INDEX

Page numbers in **boldface** are illustrations

About the Author

The award-winning author Elaine Landau has written more than three hundred books for young readers. Many of these are on health and science topics.

Landau received a bachelor's degree in English and journalism from New York University and a master's degree in library and information science from Pratt Institute. You can visit Elaine Landau at her Web site: www.elainelandau.com.